This book belongs to:

....

Using This Book

- Use the scenarios in this book as starting points for discussions with your child. Encourage them to find the picture stickers and answer the questions.

- Use the star stickers to praise and encourage their good values.

- Fill in the 'I will' tasks on the wipe-clean reward chart, and the star targets and rewards. Your child will enjoy joining in with this too, particularly in choosing the rewards. They will love the sense of responsibility, and the motivation of working towards the treats they've chosen.

- Rewards need not be big, but they should be meaningful to your child: baking a cake together, going to the swimming pool or the park, having a friend to play, a pocket money treat – something that they enjoy, and that you feel is appropriate to what they have achieved.

- Always remember to focus on their positive behaviour, and try to encourage rather than criticise. Never deny a reward that has been agreed and earned.

- Your child will soon see how developing and maintaining positive values will bring lifelong benefits to themselves and the people around them.

ISBN 978-1-78270-405-8

Copyright © Award Publications Limited

All rights reserved. No part of this publication may be reproduced or utilised in any form or by any means electronic or mechanical, including photocopying, recording, or by any information storage and retrieval system now known or hereafter invented, without the prior written permission of the publisher.

This edition first published 2025

Published by Award Publications Limited,
The Old Riding School, Welbeck,
Worksop, S80 3LR

/awardpublications @award.books
www.awardpublications.co.uk

25-1190 4

Printed in China

The Children's Book of VALUES

Sophie Giles

Illustrated by Chantal Kees and Angela Hewitt

AWARD PUBLICATIONS LIMITED

Dishonest Disaster

Connor's mum isn't happy about the mess in the living room. She asks if Connor made it, but, even though he knows he did, he denies it and blames his sister. They start to argue and are sent to their rooms.

How does Connor's dishonesty impact on others?

Honest and responsible

Connor admits he made the mess and promises that he will clear it away. He keeps his word and his mum is pleased that the living room is tidy, and very happy with Connor's honesty.

Do you always tell the truth, and keep your word?

I am honest and responsible

Not Speaking Up

Kelsey's class are on a school trip when they see another group of children. Some are in wheelchairs and others make loud noises. Kelsey's friends laugh and make unkind comments. Kelsey is embarrassed by their behaviour, but says nothing.
What should Kelsey do?

Having the Courage to Speak Up

Kelsey knows her friends are being mean and tells them to stop. They realise it is cruel to pick on others for being different, and are sorry. Their teacher overhears, and praises Kelsey for speaking out. **Are you brave enough to stand up for others?**

I am brave and speak up

No Respect

Billy and Meg are racing and jostling to be the first on the bus. They accidentally bump into a lady waiting in the queue. She stumbles and drops her shopping. The children giggle and push past her.

How are the children being disrespectful?

Respecting Others

Billy and Meg are racing to be the first on the bus. As they get to the bus stop, they see a lady waiting. They stop running and let the lady board the bus first. They offer to help her with her bags, too. She is grateful for their courtesy.
Do you show respect to others? 

I am respectful

Opting Out

Priya doesn't raise her hand to answer questions or contribute in class discussions. She's worried everyone will laugh if she gets it wrong, so she sits quietly, and lets her classmates make the effort. But she soon gets bored.

Why should Priya have a go?

Being Brave and Making an Effort

"It's OK not to know. Just be brave and have a go," encourages Priya's teacher. Priya joins in, answering and asking questions. She enjoys the class more and learns much more too.

Do you always make an effort and get involved?

I join in and try my best

Not Caring for our World

Harry can't be bothered to walk over to the litter bin, so after he finishes his snack, he drops his wrapper on the ground. He can't see the point in using the bin because the street cleaner will clear it up anyway.

How might Harry's lack of care affect others?

Looking After our Planet

When Harry finishes his snack, he puts the wrapper in his pocket until he finds a bin. He knows litter can harm wildlife and spoil our environment, and he wants to keep our planet clean and safe.

Do you care for our planet?

I care for our planet

Feeling Helpless

The play area near Jay's home is neglected and overgrown, and the equipment is scruffy and broken. He and his friends complain that they have nowhere to play outside. They stay indoors and are bored. **What can Jay do to help himself and others?**

Working Together to Make Life Better

Jay and his friends decide to tidy the play area. Soon they are working together to create a space they and others can enjoy. Everyone appreciates their hard work, and now they have a fun place to play. **Are you willing to help out to make a change?**

I enjoy working with others

Being Intolerant

Zoe notices some children get to leave their lessons early each day, including her friend Umair. "Why should they be allowed to finish before everyone else?" she thinks. This doesn't seem fair to her.

Why might Zoe think it's unfair?

Accepting Other Faiths and Beliefs

Umair can't play after school as he has to catch up on the schoolwork he misses, so he and Zoe meet on Saturdays. Zoe understands that in some religions it is important to pray at special times each day.
Do you accept the beliefs of others?

I accept the beliefs of others

Giving Up

All of Ben's friends have moved up a group in their swimming lessons, but Ben still needs to use a float, and doesn't like to put his face in the water. He feels embarrassed and asks his dad if he can stop going to the lessons.

Why is Ben keen to quit?

Being Resilient

Ben realises that if he quits, he'll never get to go in the big pool so he tries even harder. Eventually, Ben can swim confidently and goes on to join the school team. He is happy he didn't give up.
Do you keep going even when something is hard?

Not Looking Out for Others

Ella and her friends are having a great time at the park when Ella begins to feel unwell. She tells the others how she feels but they are having so much fun that they continue playing and ignore her.
Why do the other children continue their game?

Being Considerate

When Ella says she's not feeling well, her friends stop playing, and look after her. They help her sit down on the bench and give her some water. She still feels poorly, so they walk home with her.

Are you caring and considerate?

I am considerate

Judging

There's a new girl in Eva's class. Eva excitedly greets her in the playground, but the new girl doesn't reply. Eva assumes she is just being rude, so she ignores her and tells her friends the new girl is weird.

How is Eva being unkind?

Not Making Judgements

Eva greets the new girl in the playground, but when the girl replies using unfamiliar words, Eva realises that she speaks a different language. Eva thinks she might be lonely, so she makes a special effort to make friends.
Do you show kindness?

I am kind and friendly

Ignoring Others' Opinions

George's class is discussing what their school can do to help stop climate change. Everyone has lots of ideas, but George has read a lot about it, so tells everyone his ideas are best. The children start to argue. **Do you listen to what others have to say?**

Voting for a Solution

George knows that a discussion is a chance for everyone to express their opinion. He offers to make a list of all the ideas, and then everyone gets to vote to decide the actions they will all take to help.

Have you taken part in a vote?

I know about voting

Not Respecting Rules

Aria is excited to get outside to play. She knows she shouldn't, but she runs down the corridor and crashes into some younger children, knocking them over and ruining their work. They get hurt and feel upset.

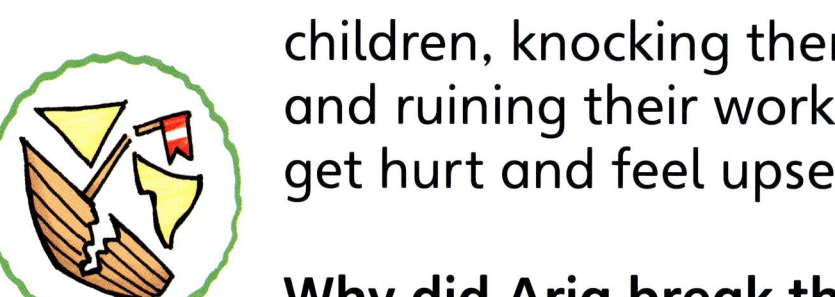

Why did Aria break the rules?

Understanding and Accepting Rules

Aria sometimes thinks rules spoil the fun, but she realises they are there for good reason to keep everyone safe. She takes care to stick to the 'no running indoors' rule and walks calmly out to the playground.

I follow the rules

Do you follow rules?

Easily Discouraged

Olivia enjoys playing on her console. She dreams of becoming a game designer, but when she tells her brother she plans to join the coding club at school to learn how, he tells her she'd find it too hard. Olivia decides not to go and gives up.
What should Olivia do?

Reaching your Goals

Olivia asks her teacher, who shows her the software they use. It's fun, and Olivia decides to join the club. Soon she is coding and making games. She knows it will help her to get her dream job, too.
Can you work towards achieving your dreams?

I work towards reaching my goals

Hogging the Limelight

At the school's special assembly, everyone is celebrating the football team winning the league. "Here's our star player and top-scorer, Rory!" says their coach. Rory grabs the trophy and raises it above his head. **How do you think Rory's teammates feel?**

Sharing the Credit

Rory knows they really won because they played as a team. "It wasn't just me," he says. "We're all star players. We worked together to defend and score." The coach smiles and agrees, praising Rory's humility. **Do you recognise everyone's efforts and share the credit?**

Glossary

We've explored lots of different values that you can practise every day. Look back through the book to see what examples you can find of each of these values.

Democracy – "rule by the people", when decisions are made by voting, rather than one person or group deciding.

Honesty – always telling the truth, doing what you say you're going to do and never lying, cheating or stealing.

Humility – being modest about what you've done, without boasting, and sharing praise fairly.

Integrity – doing the right thing, even when no one is watching.

Kindness – being gentle and considerate, and caring for others.

Openness – being willing to try new experiences, and curious about new situations and people.

Resilience – the ability to cope, adapt and keep trying even when things go wrong.

Respect – thinking and acting in a way that shows others you care about their feelings and well-being.

Encourage your child to use the picture stickers and answer the questions in the book.